MÉLANIE VIVES & RÉMI PRIEUR   ILLUSTRATED BY EL GUNTO

ESCAPE GAME

ADVENTURE

TRAPPED IN SPACE

Schiffer **Kids**™

4880 Lower Valley Road, Atglen, PA 19310

IN THE SAME COLLECTION:

Other Schiffer Books on Related Subjects:
Escape Game Adventure: The Mad Hacker, Mélanie Vives & Rémi Prieur, ISBN 978-0-7643-5896-8
Escape Game Adventure: The Last Dragon, Mélanie Vives & Rémi Prieur, ISBN 978-0-7643-5895-1
Escape Game Adventure: Operation Pizza, Mélanie Vives & Rémi Prieur, ISBN 978-0-7643-6030-5

Originally published as *Escape Game Junior: Piégés dans l'espace* © 2019 Fleurus Editions.
Translated from the French by Simulingua, Inc.

Library of Congress Control Number: 2020930737

ISBN: 978-0-7643-6031-2
Printed in China

Published by Schiffer Kids
An imprint of Schiffer Publishing, Ltd.
4880 Lower Valley Road
Atglen, PA 19310
Phone: (610) 593-1777; Fax: (610) 593-2002
E-mail: Info@schifferbooks.com
Web: www.schifferbooks.com

For our complete selection of fine books on this and related subjects, please visit our website at www.schifferbooks.com. You may also write for a free catalog.

Schiffer Publishing's titles are available at special discounts for bulk purchases for sales promotions or premiums. Special editions, including personalized covers, corporate imprints, and excerpts, can be created in large quantities for special needs. For more information, contact the publisher.

We are always looking for people to write books on new and related subjects. If you have an idea for a book, please contact us at proposals@schifferbooks.com.

WHAT IS AN ESCAPE GAME?

You must have heard of the escape game phenomenon! Life-sized "escape games" let you become bank robbers, detectives who investigate mysterious disappearances, secret agents who save the world... The idea is simple: you and your team are locked in a room, and your task is to escape by searching, solving clues, operating mechanisms... and all this in less than one hour.

Played with your family or friends, these games are intended for everyone and don't need any specific knowledge: the clues are solved by logic and team spirit. Observation, cooperation, and communication are usually the keys to success.

The first escape games appeared in 2005. They were video games played on computers. The idea was to save a person trapped in a double-locked room. One discovered object led to another to open furniture and boxes until you found the way to open the door and escape.

In Japan in 2007, an escape game was created in a real room with real objects for the first time. It is estimated that there are probably more than 10,000 escape rooms worldwide, with more than 2,300 in the United States (Source: Room Escape Artst).

IT'S YOUR TURN TO PLAY!

In a few minutes you are going to try to solve a series of clues. Remember these rules:

START TIME!

The idea is to accomplish your mission in as little time as possible. Choose your difficulty level:

 Beginner: It's the first time you played an escape game.

 Intermediate: You have already played a real escape game or did one in a book.

 Expert: You have played lots of escape games!

Start your timer after turning the next page. Or you can choose to play at your own speed!

KIT

Don't start to play without an escape gamer's basic kit: a sharp pencil and an eraser!

Write, scribble, cross out, or circle elements in the book; it will help you.

To cut out the tools on pages 43 to 48, you will also need a pair of scissors.

A GAME OF OBSERVATION

The pages with a green disc around the number aren't read in the traditional way, from page 13 to 14 (for example): it's only by carefully observing and solving the clues that you'll find a number that will direct you to the page where the next part of the adventure continues. Don't cheat and leaf through the book randomly: you should only turn to a page if you have found the solution that takes you there!

If you are at a page with a dog-eared corner, you can read another page: the following one if the right-hand corner is dog-eared, the preceding page if the left-hand corner is dog-eared.

CHECK YOUR ANSWERS

Each time you think you've found the answer to a puzzle, you should check your answer! Turn to page 42 and ask Dooz the robot, your faithful friend, to help you read the validation grid.

DOOZ'S TOOLBOX

Dooz the robot is there to help you.

Before starting your mission, he will give you some objects that will help to solve some clues. Go quickly to pages 43–48 and cut them out!

NEED SOME HELP?

During the adventures, you are the game master. If you really can't solve a clue, you can always ask Dooz for a hint (orange pages 30–35), or the complete answer (purple pages 36–41). Unlike the clues, the help system follows the correct order of the pages: you will find one or more hints and one solution for each page. For example, if you are stuck on page 26, see the hint that corresponds to that page.

Don't feel guilty about having a look at the hints: remember that they are a part of the game and that it's normal, just like in a real escape game room, to ask for help.

IN THIS BOOK

START TIME!

Welcome!

You are a member of the Spatial-Temporal Agency Y, where you are a specialist at high-risk missions: whenever there is a need, the agency can call you and send you out to put things right at any moment in time. Blocking a terrible attack by an enemy in 1917? Catching an escaped criminal in 1541? Recovering a magic amulet in prehistoric times? They always call you!

Luckily, Agency Y never sends you on a mission alone: Dooz, your faithful robot, always goes with you. It's thanks to his time-travel portal that you can travel through time. Beware: you need to reach your objective as quickly as possible because Dooz can't keep the portal active over a long period of time.

Today, your mission will send you to 3144. A team of astronauts from the planet Vacumy, who went on an exploration aboard a space shuttle, have not responded for twenty-four hours. The Vacumians, a good and generous people, have always been in the sights of the diabolical inhabitants of the star Hyena ... If anything has happened to these astronauts, who are among the most brilliant scientists of their time, the Hyenas are probably responsible. You have to intervene fast!

You must enter the ship to find out what happened to the crew members, rescue them if necessary, and escort them safely back to their planet.

Quick, turn the page!

DO YOU KNOW?

The word SPACE refers to everything that begins beyond the atmosphere, the layer of gas that surrounds and protects the Earth. We generally consider that we are in space as soon as we cross the Karman line, which is at an altitude of sixty-two miles. It was a Russian, Yuri Gagarin, who was the first to go there, on April 12, 1961, aboard his capsule "Vostok 1."

Dooz and his time-travel portal just dropped you off in space, in front of the space shuttle's entrance airlock. Find a way to get aboard!

8

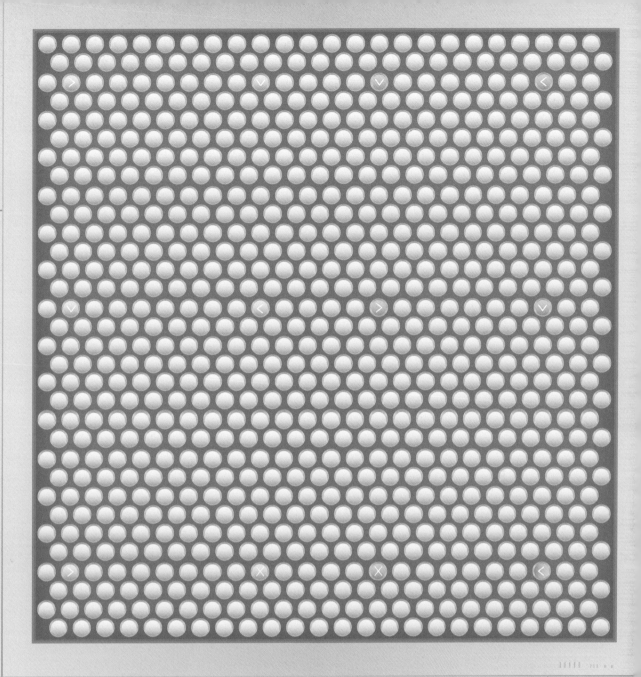

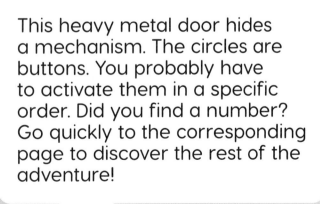

This heavy metal door hides a mechanism. The circles are buttons. You probably have to activate them in a specific order. Did you find a number? Go quickly to the corresponding page to discover the rest of the adventure!

YOUR ANSWER

....

Well done! You now know which antidote to use! You rush to the infirmary, but the pharmaceutical fridge is locked by a digicode.

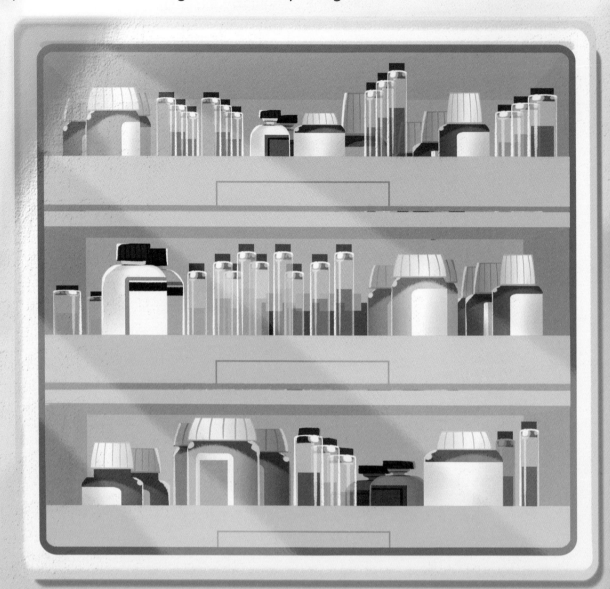

DO YOU KNOW?

In the ISS, the International Space Station, there is no SHOWER OR WASHING MACHINE! Astronauts wash themselves with wet wipes and wash their hair with dry shampoo. Cleaning clothes would consume too much water, so they wear their clothes as long as possible: up to a week for socks.

Look carefully at the keys: the last person who typed the code did not bother to wash their hands . . . When you find your answer, jump ahead that number of pages.

YOUR ANSWER

....

You've set everything right, yet the shuttle won't move. You just noticed that a red light is flashing: it seems that the left wing has a mechanical problem! Someone must be assigned to doing the repairs outside . . .

I'll go; it's too dangerous for you! But I can't go out like this; you have to help me.

YOUR ANSWER

....

DO YOU KNOW?

Inside a space station, there is no need for a SPACE SUIT. On the other hand, astronauts must wear them when venturing outdoors to perform repairs or take samples: they provide oxygen, remove carbon dioxide, and maintain a comfortable temperature. In space, it can drop to -454°F!

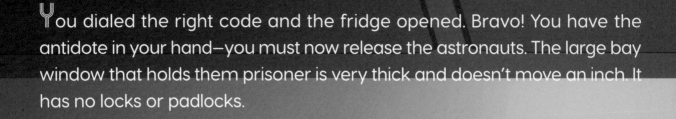

You dialed the right code and the fridge opened. Bravo! You have the antidote in your hand—you must now release the astronauts. The large bay window that holds them prisoner is very thick and doesn't move an inch. It has no locks or padlocks.

I think we can hack into the system by using our magnetic hacking cards! Let's synchronize: I placed mine on the electrical box; now you do the same.

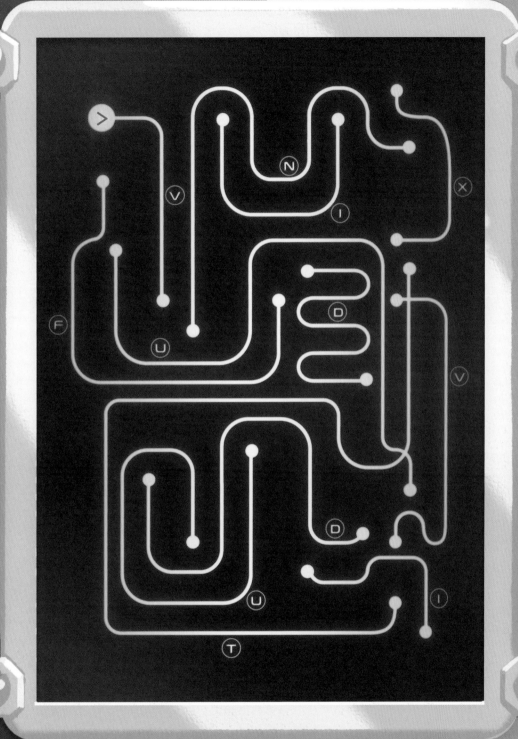

YOUR ANSWER

....

15

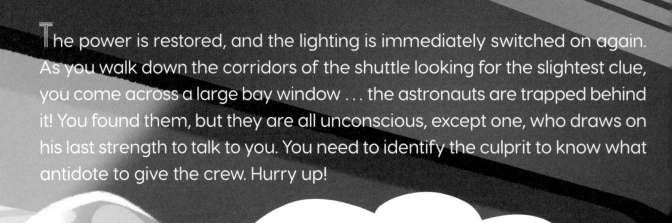

The power is restored, and the lighting is immediately switched on again. As you walk down the corridors of the shuttle looking for the slightest clue, you come across a large bay window … the astronauts are trapped behind it! You found them, but they are all unconscious, except one, who draws on his last strength to talk to you. You need to identify the culprit to know what antidote to give the crew. Hurry up!

A creature sent by the inhabitants of Hyena attacked us and contaminated us. Just before, I was able to activate a protective spray, but it wasn't enough …

YOUR ANSWER

....

WANTED

DANGER

DO NOT APPROACH THESE CREATURES
UNDER ANY CIRCUMSTANCES

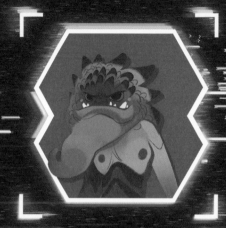

IDENTITY:
PIPWRB ANTIDOTE NO: **22**

IDENTITY:
HQJPWK ANTIDOTE NO: **29**

IDENTITY:
FMDTSW ANTIDOTE NO: **34**

IDENTITY:
APNUVT ANTIDOTE NO: **14**

IDENTITY:
FDXJWD ANTIDOTE NO: **10**

IDENTITY:
LRHRDJ ANTIDOTE NO: **27**

Congratulations! Mission accomplished: Dooz fixed the shuttle's wing and you finally made it to the planet Vacumy, where the welcome was triumphant. Thanks to you, the astronauts escaped the clutches of Hyena's fierce creature! For saving their brilliant scientists, the Vacumians will be eternally grateful to you.

Dooz seems to be very proud of you. Your robot brings you back to reality by creating a time-travel portal. It's time to go back to the present day! But not for long, because Dooz has warned you: a new mission is waiting for you . . .

Sparks suddenly burst out of the electrical box and the window slides out. You did it: the way is clear! All you have to do now is inject the antidote into the crew members. As they gradually come to their senses, a thumping noise makes you jump. The creature is still aboard the ship, facing you . . .

We'll be stronger together! Attack!

YOUR ANSWER

DO YOU KNOW?

Since LIFE exists on Earth, it is quite possible that it is present on other planets, within solar systems other than ours! But many conditions need to be met: the planet must not be too big or too small, for example, and it must be at a safe distance from its star so that it is neither too hot nor too cold. The research continues . . .

23

You're inside. Congratulations! There is no noise and the shuttle is plunged into darkness. First, you need to get the power back on.

24

The creature is defeated; this time no one was hurt! It's time to return to the planet Vacumy. The astronauts are not yet in a position to program the shuttle; you're going to have to do it . . . There are four steps to follow.

SHIP X135-B STABILIZED
DESTINATION: PLANET VACUMY

TURBULENCE ZONES DETECTED
POSTING ADVISED ITINERARY:

> PASS IN FRONT OF ZOLTA 30
> REJOIN CORIFRON
> GO ALONG THE PLANETARY SYSTEM UNTIL
YOU REACH THE GREAT BORE
> REJOIN YU
> CONTINUE TO ZOLTA 35
> CONTINUE TO VACUMY

4 13 21 29 37

TURBO POWER

1 3 7 5

ENGINE PRESSURE

0 1 2 3 4 5 6

OIL LEVEL

750
500
1000
250
0

START

STOP

1 2 3 4 5

IGNITION REACTORS

VALIDATION

Max.

0
1
2
3
4
5
6
7

10	22	26	⚠	29	⏻	69	2	⚠	19
14	21	⏻	41	72	19	41	63	48	24
38	⚠	72	⏻	39	⚠	56	⚠	71	37
44	51	23	⚠	18	19	27	⏻	68	29
37	11	⚠	37	99	⚠	52	33	29	⚠
5	11	56	27	⏻	7	!	14	83	33
⏻	20	✳	✳	24	13	88	21	⚠	41
62	31	78	44	19	⏻	53	⏻	32	52

YOUR ANSWER STARTS THE SHIP:

The hints are listed by page and not by the solving order of the clues. If you need a helping hand, go read the hints that are associated with the page you are stuck on!

PAGES 8-9

HINT 1: Focus on the metal door in front of you ... Even if your brain only shows a few colored circles at the same time, it has twelve! Six green circles and six pink circles.

HINT 2: Have you spotted all the colored circles? You probably have to connect them in a certain way ... Have you noticed that they contain arrows?

HINT 3: How about trying to connect the circles of the same color by following the arrows? For example, if a green circle contains an arrow to the right, from this circle, trace a line to the right until you meet another green circle ...

HINT 4: Did you manage to connect all the green circles? If so, you must have drawn a 2. You'll find a second number thanks to the pink circles! Don't forget to check your answer on Dooz's validation grid on page 42.

HINT 1: Look at the fingerprints: they all look different. This could help you find out in which order the keys were typed...

HINT 2: The person who typed the code certainly left a lot of dirt on the first key he pressed, then a little less on the next key, and even less on the next one...

HINT 3: Do you know in which order the keys were activated? Did you notice that each key typed corresponds to several letters? For example, key 3 can correspond to a D, an E, an F... You probably have to find a word!

HINT 4:

> According to my information, the first letter is F.

You think you found the right code? Check your answer as soon as possible using Dooz's validation grid on page 42.

HINT 1: Did you take a good look at the items Dooz gave you before the mission began? You can cut them out on pages 43 to 48. Some will probably help you!

HINT 2: Dress Dooz with the right equipment! You can cut out accessories and clothing on pages 43 to 44.

HINT 3: The equipment you need to choose for Dooz consists of three different parts. Select the right clothes and accessories and prepare a complete outfit for him. Be careful—some seem damaged—wearing them outside the ship would be dangerous...

HINT 4: You have equipped Dooz with the right equipment and he is now ready to carry out the external repair. Take a good look at his equipment; it is hiding two figures... Don't hesitate for a second: check your answer using Dooz's validation grid on page 42.

HINT 1: Remember that a dog-eared corner of a page gives you access to the next or previous page!

HINT 2: Did you take a good look at the objects that Dooz entrusted to you before the beginning of the mission? You can cut them out on pages 43 to 48. One of them will help you!

HINT 3: Dooz has placed his magnetic card on the electrical box on page 15. You can get yours on pages 45 to 46, then place it on page 16! Be careful not to make a mistake: once the card is placed there, the printed circuit board must face you, and you must be able to read the letters on it.

HINT 4: Do you see the orange arrow drawn on Dooz's map on page 15? Why don't you try following the cable from this arrow?

HINT 5: The cable goes into Dooz's magnetic card and reappears on yours, just behind, on the back! Then it reappears again on Dooz's, and vice versa. Follow the cable from page 15 to page 16 and vice versa, until you reach a green cross.

HINT 6: By following the cable from the arrow to the cross, you will recover several letters that, in order, form a word... You can check your answer on Dooz's validation grid, page 42!

HINT 1: When the astronaut speaking to you triggered his protective jet, the creature's silhouette formed on the glass. Observe it carefully...

The silhouette obviously must be that of a creature that appears on the WANTED notice.

HINT 2: Did you find out which creature matches the silhouette that formed on the glass? In that case, you know which antidote to use to treat the crew! It corresponds to a number. Check your answer on Dooz's validation grid on page 42!

PAGES 20-21

No hints for these pages.

PAGES 22-23

HINT 1: Did you take a good look at the items Dooz gave you before the mission began? You can cut them out on pages 43 to 48. Some will probably help you!

HINT 2: You and Dooz must attack the creature with sabers! You can cut them out on pages 45 to 46.

HINT 3:

 Have you noticed the red dot and the blue dot that appear on the creature's body? It is probably precisely on these points that we must place the sabers!

HINT 4: Put the end of the red lightsaber on the red dot, and the end of the blue lightsaber on the blue dot, flat on the page. Then, rotate the two sabers around these points, until a number appears . . .

HINT 5: The first number, the one that appears on the left, is a 2. You just have to decipher the second . . . Quickly check your answer on Dooz's validation grid on page 42!

HINT 1: Of all the cables, only two seem to be in working order: you must connect these two cables! The others are all damaged ...

HINT 2:

Have you noticed that a number is written on the end of each cable?

HINT 3: Have you located the two outlets where you need to make the connections? From left to right, the first one is blue, the second one is red ... By plugging the correct cables into the correct sockets, you will get a two-digit number. Go check your answer using Dooz's validation grid on page 42!

HINT 1: Remember that a dog-eared corner of a page gives you access to the next or previous page!

HINT 2: Did you take a good look at the objects that Dooz entrusted to you before the beginning of the mission? You can cut them out on pages 43 to 48. One of them will help you!

HINT 3: To program the shuttle, you must follow four steps. Each page allows you to make one. The instruction manual "Programming the X135-B Ship," to be cut out on pages 47 to 48, will be essential for you.

HINT 4: For the first part, on page 26, read the itinerary carefully on the dashboard screen. Starting from the shuttle, on the left, trace the route that will take you to Vacumy! Thanks to the reminder in the instruction manual, you know what the planets you have to pass look like.

HINT 5: Did you complete this first step? Your line must draw a number! Put it aside; you'll need it once you've completed the four steps.

HINT 6: For the second step, on page 27 carefully follow the instructions in the section "Motor Settings" on the instruction manual. Thanks to this, you will be able to deduce which numbered button to press. Be careful, you only have to press one of the five buttons! Which one did you find? So you got a number back. Put it aside; you'll need it once you've completed the four steps.

HINT 7: For the third step, on page 28 you must fill the fuel gauge to the maximum level. Notch 1 of the knob fills the gauge with one unit of fuel, notch 2 with two units of fuel, etc. To find out how many units you need to add, use the empty gauge drawn on the instruction manual! Put it alongside the gauge and count the number of missing units. Be careful; the gauge is already filled with 2 units.

HINT 8: Have you completed this third step? The number of units to be added corresponds to the number on which you have to set the knob, so it is the number you're looking for! Put it aside; you'll need it once you've completed the four steps.

HINT 9: For the fourth step, on page 29 carefully follow the instructions in the paragraph "Setting the Autopilot" in the instruction manual. Don't hesitate to use a pencil to cross out all the buttons you activate; you'll see more clearly!

HINT 10: Have you completed this fourth step? The buttons that are not activated seem to draw a number . . . This is the fourth number you are looking for! If you have completed the four steps and therefore recovered four numbers, you now have everything you need to start the ship . . .

HINT 11: Have you noticed that each step is represented by a small symbol? Four pages, four steps, four symbols, four numbers . . . You will find these symbols at the bottom of page 29, next to the inscription "Start the ship."

HINT 12: Have you done the math and retrieved a two-digit number? Quickly go check your answer on Dooz's validation grid on page 42!

ANSWERS

The answers are listed by page and not by the solving order of the clues. If you need a helping hand, go ahead and read the solution that is associated with the page you are stuck on!

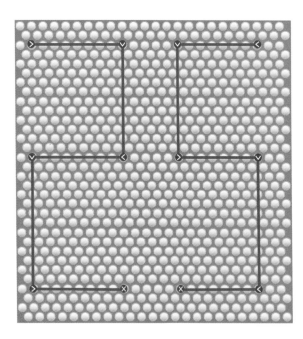

PAGES 8-9

Even if your brain doesn't see more than a few colored circles simultaneously, the metal door in front of you has twelve: six green and six red. Connect the circles of the same color by following the arrows! For example, if a green circle contains an arrow to the right, starting from this circle, trace a line to the right until you meet another green circle . . . You will get the result shown opposite. Your line draws the number 25! Why don't you go to page 25 as soon as possible to enter the space shuttle. The rest of the adventure awaits you there!

PAGES 10-11

The person who typed the code left a lot of dirt on the first key he pressed, then a little less on the next key, and even less on the next one, etc. So you know he pressed key 3, then key 6, key 8, and finally key 7.

Look closely at the digicode: each of these keys corresponds to several letters!

The 3 key can correspond to a D, E, F.

The 6 key can correspond to an M, N, or O, etc.

The last person to open the pharmaceutical fridge could only dial one word: "FOUR."

Every second counts, so quickly jump ahead four pages!

PAGES 12-13

Cut out the accessories and clothes from Dooz's toolbox, pages 43 to 44, and dress your robot with the right equipment! Be careful—some seem damaged—wearing them outside the ship would be dangerous ... Choose them carefully and prepare a complete outfit for him. You will get the outfit on the left. Look at his equipment; it's hiding two numbers! So you will find, from top to bottom, a "2" and then a "1." Go quickly to page 21 so that Dooz can do the repairs outside!

PAGES 14-17

Dooz put his magnetic card on the electrical box on page 15. Cut yours out of the toolbox on pages 45 to 46, then put it on page 16! Don't make a mistake: once the card is placed, the printed circuit board must face you, and you must be able to read the letters on it. Then look at the map held by Dooz on page 15 and follow the cable from the orange arrow. It goes into Dooz's magnetic card and reappears on yours, right behind it, on the back! Then it reappears again on Dooz's, and vice versa. Follow the cable from page 15 to page 16 and vice versa until you reach a green cross.

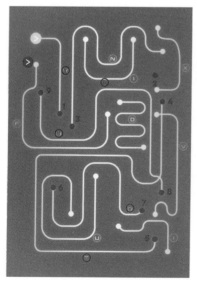
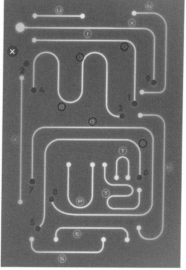

page 15 >   < page 16

Following the arrow cable to the cross, you have retrieved several letters that, in order, form a word: you have passed over a "T," then a "W," an "E," an "N," a "T," a "Y," then a "T," a "W," and an "O." You found the word "TWENTY-TWO"! Go to page 22 to activate the magnetic hacking cards and experience the rest of the adventure!

PAGES 18-19

The silhouette formed on the glass is that of a creature that appears on the WANTED notice. You identified which creature attacked the crew, so you know what antidote to use to cure them! On the WANTED notice, under the guilty creature, you can read: "Antidote No. 10." There is not a minute to lose! Go quickly to page 10 to go to the infirmary...

PAGES 22-23

You and Dooz must attack the creature with sabers! Cut them out from the toolbox on pages 45 to 46. On the creature's body, a red dot and a blue dot appear: it is precisely on these points that the sabers must be placed. Point the end of the red saber at the red point, and the end of the blue saber at the blue point, flat on the page. Then rotate the two swords around at these points, until a number emerges... You will get this result:

You have formed the number 27. So go as fast as you can to page 27 and attack the creature. Time is running out!

PAGES 24-25

Of all the cables, only two are in working order: the blue cable with the number 1 on the end and the red cable with the number 8 on the end. Have you located the two outlets where you need to make the connections? From left to right, the first one is blue, the second one is red . . . To turn the power back on, you have to plug the blue cable with the number 1 into the blue socket, then the red cable with the number 8 into the red socket. So you just got the number 18 back! Go quickly to page 18 to discover the rest of your mission!

PAGES 26-29

To program the shuttle, you must follow four steps. Each page allows you to complete one. Cut out the instruction manual "Programming the X135-B Ship" from Dooz's toolbox on pages 47 to 48: you will need it!

First step, page 26:

Read carefully the itinerary indicated on the dashboard screen. From the shuttle, on the left, make your way to Vacumy! Thanks to the reminder in the instruction manual, you know what the planets you have to go past look like. You will discover this:

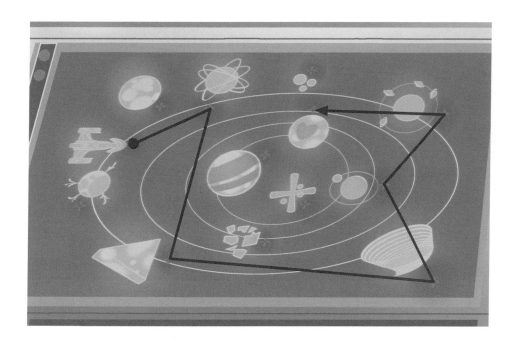

The line draws a 13! So you found the number 13. Put it aside; you'll need it once you've completed the four steps.

Second step, page 27:
Carefully follow the instructions in the "Engine Settings" section of the instruction manual and you will deduce which numbered button to press!

• "If the turbo power is less than 500 decatons, press the first of the five buttons": the turbo power is greater than 500 decatones, so you should not press the button.

• "If the turbo power has only odd numbers, don't press on the middle button": the turbo power has only odd numbers, so you shouldn't press the button.

• "If the oil gauge indicates a value below 500, do not switch on the second button from the right": the oil gauge indicates a value below 500, so do not press the button.

• "If more than two reactors are on, do not press the button with the number 4": three reactors are on, so you should not press the button.

• "If the validation button is yellow, do not press the yellow button": the validation button is yellow, so you should not press on the yellow button.

By elimination, you must therefore press the orange button, which is number 13. You found the number 13. Put it aside; you'll need it once you've completed the four steps.

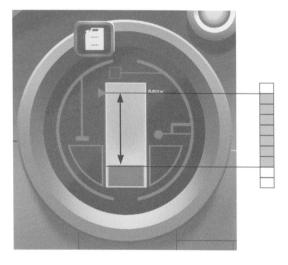

Third step, page 28:
You must fill the fuel gauge to the maximum level. Notch 1 of the knob fills the gauge with one unit of fuel, notch 2 with two units of fuel, etc. To know how many units you need to add, use the empty gauge drawn on the manual instructions! Place it along the gauge and count the number of missing units. Be careful! The gauge is already filled to two units. To fill the gauge to maximum, you must add seven units of fuel. So that's the number you have to set the knob to. You found the number 7! Put it aside; you'll need it once the four steps are completed.

Fourth step, page 29:

Carefully follow the instructions in the "Autopilot Setting" section of the instruction manual. With a pencil, cross out all the buttons you activate so you will see more clearly! The buttons that are not activated draw a 7: so you found the number 7!

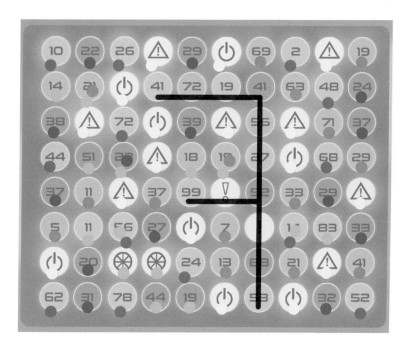

How to start the ship?

You have completed the four steps and therefore retrieved four numbers. You now have everything you need to start the ship ... At the bottom of page 29, next to the inscription "Start the ship," you can see a mathematical equation:

Each symbol corresponds to a step you have completed, and therefore to a number that you found!

On page 26, you see the symbol ♀, which corresponds to step 1, "configuring the itinerary." During this step, you recovered a 13.

On page 27, you see the symbol 📷, which corresponds to step 2, "engine settings." During this step, you recovered a 13.

On page 28, you see the symbol 📋, which corresponds to step 3, "fuel level check." During this step, you recovered a 7.

On page 29, you see the symbol 🚀, which corresponds to step 4, "setting the automatic pilot." During this step, you recovered a 7.

13+13-7-7 = 12. Hurry up and go to page 12 to start the ship!

Have you found the right answer to a clue?

To find out, ask Dooz the robot! He managed to find a grid that will allows you to check each answer.

HOW TO USE IT: For example, if you think the solution to the puzzle on pages 24 to 25 is 19, look for the column "pages 24–25" and the row "19." If, where the two meet, you see a "thumbs up" sign, it means that you have found the correct answer and you can go to page 19, where the next part of the mission is waiting for you!

PAGES OF THE CLUES TO BE SOLVED

PAGE WHERE THE NEXT STAGE OF THE MISSION IS TO BE FOUND

	8-9	10-11	12-13	14-17	18-19	22-23	24-25	26-29
9	👎	👎	👎	👎	👎	👎	👎	👎
10	👎	👎	👎	👎	👍	👎	👎	👎
11	👎	👎	👎	👎	👎	👎	👎	👎
12	👎	👎	👎	👎	👎	👎	👎	👍
13	👎	👎	👎	👎	👎	👎	👎	👎
14	👎	👎	👎	👎	👎	👎	👎	👎
15	👎	👍	👎	👎	👎	👎	👎	👎
16	👎	👎	👎	👎	👎	👎	👎	👎
17	👎	👎	👎	👎	👎	👎	👎	👎
18	👎	👎	👎	👎	👎	👎	👍	👎
19	👎	👎	👎	👎	👎	👎	👎	👎
20	👎	👎	👎	👎	👎	👎	👎	👎
21	👎	👎	👍	👎	👎	👎	👎	👎
22	👎	👎	👎	👍	👎	👎	👎	👎
23	👎	👎	👎	👎	👎	👎	👎	👎
24	👎	👎	👎	👎	👎	👎	👎	👎
25	👍	👎	👎	👎	👎	👎	👎	👎
26	👎	👎	👎	👎	👎	👎	👎	👎
27	👎	👎	👎	👎	👎	👍	👎	👎
28	👎	👎	👎	👎	👎	👎	👎	👎
29	👎	👎	👎	👎	👎	👎	👎	👎
30	👎	👎	👎	👎	👎	👎	👎	👎
31	👎	👎	👎	👎	👎	👎	👎	👎

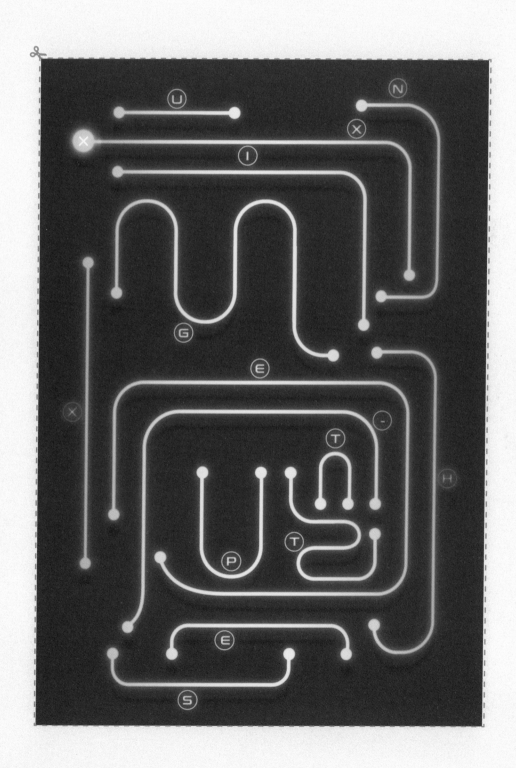

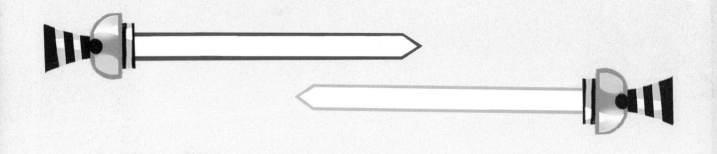

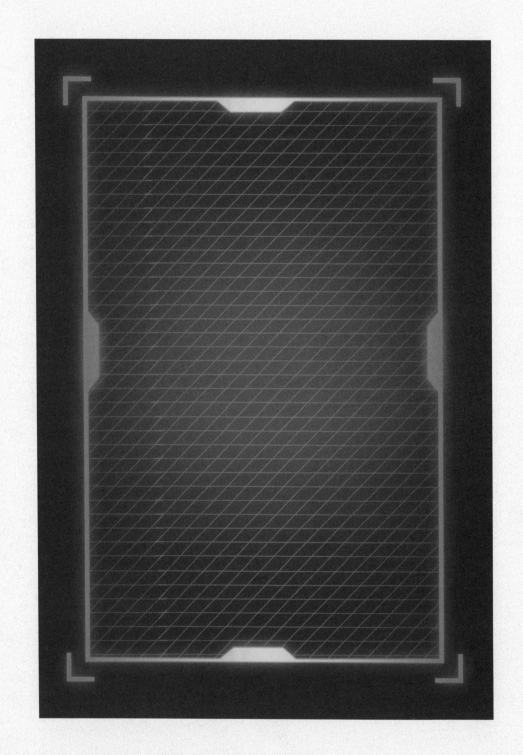

PROGRAMMING THE X135-B SHIP

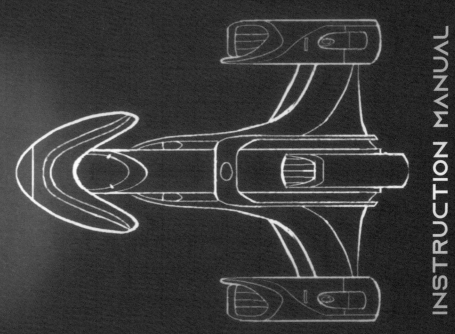

INSTRUCTION MANUAL

STEP 1 CONFIGURING THE ITINERARY

To configure your itinerary, follow the instructions display on the instrument panel's screen

Memo board:

Zolta 25 has a propeller structure

Zolta 30 is also called "the planet with four rings"

Zolta 35 each of its four moons has a ring

Corifron is also called "the triangular planet"

Corifron 2 is also called "the rectangular planet"

Vacumy is a round planet easily identifiable due to its heart-shaped lake

Yu is easily spotted due to its single moon that revolves around it

STEP 2 ENGINE SETTINGS

To set the engines, you need to engage just one of the five numbered, colored buttons:

> If the turbo power is less than 500 decatons, press the first of the five buttons.

> If the turbo power has only odd numbers, don't press on the middle button.

> If the oil gauge indicates a value below 500, do not switch on the second button from the right.

> If more than two reactors are on, do not press the button with the number 4.

> If the validation button is yellow, do not press the yellow button.

STEP 3 FUEL LEVEL CHECK

Fill the gauge to the maximum level.
To do this, set the dial to the line corresponding to the amount of fuel you need to add.
The first line indicates one unit of fuel, the second line indicates two units, etc.

I‾ unit

STEP 4 SETTING THE AUTOMATIC PILOT

> Activate all the blue buttons that have an even number.

> Activate all the yellow buttons that have the symbols needed ▲ and ⏻.

> Activate all the red buttons that have a number between 20 and 40.

> Activate all the green buttons that have an odd number.

> If two buttons side by side are the same color, activate both of them, no matter the number or symbol on them, unless they are diagonal.

Hint:

It would be easier for you if you cross out the buttons you want to activate as you go along.